the dubious dolphin dilemma

a delaware beach mystery

Denise Blum   Lisa Sanderson

Written by Denise Blum. Illustrated by Melissa Walters.

Printed in the USA.

Mainstay Publishing
P.O. Box 293
Middletown, DE 19709
(302) 223-6636
publisher@mainstaypublishing.com
www.mainstaypublishing.com

ISBN 978-0-9832901-0-0

"OOOOOOOhhhhh
NNNNNOOOO!!!!!!"

Where is it? Where is it? Where could it be?
The most fabulous toy in all history!!!
My favorite stuffed dolphin with blue button eyes.
Aunt Cass gave him to me. It was a surprise!

Where did I lose him? What did I do?
Is he in Daddy's car? Or uncle Ed's shoe?

MOOOOOOOOOOOOMMMMYYYYYY!

Help me, please help me.
My Dolphin is gone.
Let's go on a search to find him.
Come on!

We must track him, retrieve him, we'll hunt 'til we drop.
Could he be at the park? Is he at Sea Shell Shop?

It's a mystery, says mom, detectives we'll be.
Look high and look low, we'll find him, you'll see.
We'll solve this case as we search for a clue.
We'll study, we'll probe, we'll investigate too.
DETECTIVE JOURNAL

Readers, will you help us?
Make a notation.
The pictures have clues
to Dolphin's location.

Be a detective, a sleuth,
and help solve the case.
Look for evidence, a hint,
a tip or a trace.

Let's retrace your steps,
You spent time with Aunt cass.
Did you go to the mountains,
did you hike through the grass?

Our first stop was Lewes, so fun to explore!
We took a long walk down the sparkling seashore.

We went surf fishing and used squid for bait.
Caught one baby shark and one giant skate.

Is my dolphin at Kids Ketch
beside the blue train?
Is he next to a puppet
or model airplane?
KIDS' KETCH
TOYS & FASHIONS
CHEF
TIME
CANCEL
START

Rocky Mountain chocolate could be the place
Where we find my dolphin and solve this case!

Is he covered in fudge from his tail to his head?
Or under a caramel apple instead?

As detectives we need to follow the clues.
Do you think my dolphin's at Bethany Blues?

We stopped for a snack. The ribs were divine.
Aunt Cass ate all hers and then tried to steal mine!

On to Rehoboth, with so much to see!
The whole town was bustling with activity.

We rode bikes on the boardwalk, then browsed through the shops.
I bought a red t-shirt and brand new flip flops.

The seagulls were circling, we gave them some bread.

What a mistake! One splattered my head!

We stopped at Dos Locos for some Stonegrill steak.
Did I leave my dolphin there by mistake?

As I ate my fried ice cream, did he fall to the floor?
Is he under a taco or next to the door?

Sea Shell Shop, on Rehoboth Avenue, was filled with fun gear.
Did I leave my dolphin next to the cashier?

I bought two hermit crabs and a pretty conch shell.
A book, yummy fudge and a shiny ship's bell!

Our tummies were grumbling so quick as a mouse
we went to Henlopen City Oyster House.

The seafood was fresh, caught that very same day
When the chef turned his back, it all got away!

Boardwalk Plaza Hotel is where we spent the night.
The beds were so comfy, the pillows just right.

It's a dubious dilemma. I must solve this case!
How could he vanish without a trace?

The next day we woke up to blue skies and bright sun.
The perfect conditions to have some more fun!

We went offshore fishing way out in the ocean.
Aunt Cass got seasick from all of the motion!

When we got back, it was time for lunch.
I wanted a tasty snack to munch.

Grotto is legendary down at the beach.
We stopped in for pizza, two slices each!

Is my dolphin at Sea Shell Shop, out on Route one?
Or at Shell We Golf, where we had so much fun?

They had lighthouses, pendants and clocks trimmed in chrome.
Aunt Cass bought a table and lamp for her home!

We traveled to Dewey and soaked in some sun.
Then went windsurfing. Boy was that fun!

We tried boogie boards and had high expectations.
But riding the waves brought a few complications!

Another fun stop on our beach vacation
Was the Indian River Life Saving Station.

We learned about shipwrecks and keepers and crews
And how surfmen saved sailors in many rescues.

Is my dolphin at Fifer's, did he fall in a pie?
Is he under a sandwich that's thirteen feet high?

Is he covered in peaches, so juicy and sweet?
Beneath an apple or fruit smoothie treat?

Bethany was next, we took a long stroll.
We passed the golf course and big totem pole.
Readers, are you looking for clues?

In Fenwick, the lighthouse stands bold and tall.
Did I drop my dolphin next to the wall?

We watched as a surfer caught a huge wave.
Then did a 360, man, he was brave!

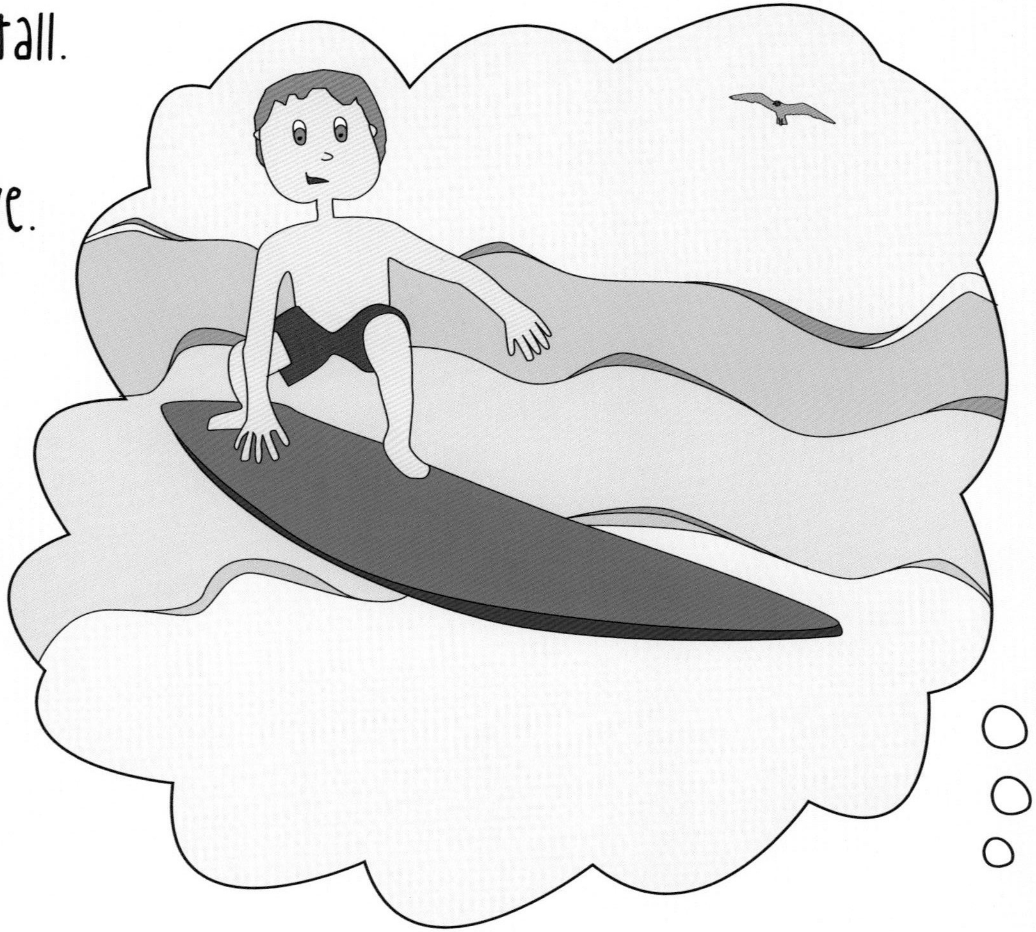

It was the end of the day, it was time to relax.
We paddled through creeks in yellow kayaks.
When we were done, we took a quick dip.
Then headed home for the end of our trip.

Mom says as she hugs me
and tickles my toes,
The mystery's been solved.
The case is now closed.

My dolphin is back!
What a wonderful day!
The Delaware beaches...
a great place to play!

To "my favorites" - Chris, Chase and Cassidy - Thank you for your love and support. I smile everyday because of you! -D.B.

To Sean, Ty & Molly - I love you so much. Always lots of laughter in our house! -L.S.

To my family and friends- thanks for always being there! -M.W.

To Murk - We're still walking fast! Thanks for everything! - L.S. & D.B.